P9-BJF-122

ALSO BY

Florence Parry Heide

Tales for the Perfect Child

Fables
You
Shouldn't
Pay Any
Attention To

Fables You Shouldn't Pay Any Attention To

Florence Parry Heide and

Sylvia Worth Van Clief

Illustrated by Sergio Ruzzier

atheneum

ATHENEUM BOOKS FOR YOUNG READERS
New York London Toronto Sydney New Delhi

Fables
You
Shouldn't
Pay Any
Attention To

ATHENEUM BOOKS FOR YOUNG READERS
An imprint of Simon & Schuster Children's Publishing Division
1230 Avenue of the Americas, New York, New York 10020

This book is a work of fiction. Any references to historical events, real people,
or real places are used fictitiously. Other names, characters, places, and events
are products of the author's imagination, and any resemblance to actual events
or places or persons, living or dead, is entirely coincidental.
Text copyright © 1978 by Florence Parry Heide and William C. Van Clief III
"Phoebe" and "Sally" text copyright © 2017 by The Florence P. Heide
Irrevocable Trust and William C. Van Clief Trust
Illustrations copyright © 2017 by Sergio Ruzzier
A different version of this work was originally published in 1978 by
J.B. Lippincott Company
All rights reserved, including the right of reproduction in whole or in part
in any form.
ATHENEUM BOOKS FOR YOUNG READERS is a registered trademark
of Simon & Schuster, Inc.
Atheneum logo is a trademark of Simon & Schuster, Inc.

For information about special discounts for bulk purchases, please
contact Simon & Schuster Special Sales at 1-866-506-1949 or
business@simonandschuster.com.
The Simon & Schuster Speakers Bureau can bring authors to your live event.
For more information or to book an event, contact the
Simon & Schuster Speakers Bureau at 1-866-248-3049 or visit
our website at www.simonspeakers.com.
Book design by Debra Sfetsios-Conover
The text for this book was set in Sabon.
The illustrations for this book were rendered in pen & ink and ink wash
on paper.
Manufactured in the United States of America   0617 FFG
This Atheneum Books for Young Readers edition July 2017
10 9 8 7 6 5 4 3 2 1
Library of Congress Cataloging-in-Publication Data
Names: Heide, Florence Parry, author. | Van Clief, Sylvia Worth, author.
Ruzzier, Sergio, 1966- illustrator.
Title: Fables you shouldn't pay any attention to / Florence Parry Heide
and Sylvia Worth Van Clief ; illustrated by Sergio Ruzzier.
Other titles: Fables you should not pay any attention to
Description: New York : Atheneum Books for Young Readers, [2017] | First
published in 1978. | Summary: Brief tales extolling the "virtues" of carelessness,
greed, lying, selfishness, and other "admirable" qualities.
Identifiers: LCCN 2015043367
Subjects: LCSH: Conduct of life—Juvenile fiction. | Children's stories,
American | CYAC: Conduct of life—Fiction. | Short stories. Classification: LCC
PZ7.H36 Fab 2017 | DDC [Fic]—dc23
LC record available at https://lccn.loc.gov/2015043367
ISBN 978-1-4814-6382-9 (hc)   ISBN 978-1-4814-6384-3 (eBook)

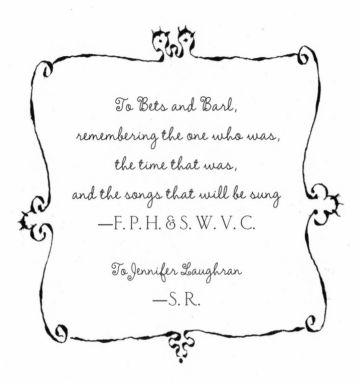

To Bets and Barl,
remembering the one who was,
the time that was,
and the songs that will be sung
—F. P. H. & S. W. V. C.

To Jennifer Laughran
—S. R.

CONTENTS

Genevieve

GENEVIEVE WAS CARELESS.

Isn't that terrible? She was very,
very careless.

All the other children took off
their good clothes and put on their

old play clothes when they went outside to play.

But not Genevieve. She played in her very best dresses. So all of her very best dresses were dirty and stained and torn.

All the other children were very careful with their toys. They always put them away when they were through playing. Their dolls and trucks and bikes and games were just like new. They never got lost. They never got broken. They never got wet. They never wore out.

But Genevieve was very, very careless with her toys. She left her bike outside to get rusty. Her doll was in terrible shape. *All* of her toys were in terrible shape. The ones that weren't broken were wet. The ones that weren't broken or wet were lost.

Oh, Genevieve was careless, all right.

When Christmastime came near, her father and mother sat down to make out a Christmas list.

"None of the children really needs a thing," said her mother. "Their clothes are just like new.

Their toys are just like new. But Genevieve needs all new dresses. And Genevieve needs all new toys."

So that year the other children got very little for Christmas.

Genevieve got all new clothes and all new toys.

It pays to be careless, thought Genevieve, as she rode her beautiful new bike around the block.

Phoebe

ALL THE BEES WERE BUSY AS
bees. All but Phoebe.

She always put off until tomorrow what she should be doing
today.

"You're going to ruin our reputation," said the other bees. "People always say 'busy as bees' because bees are supposed to be busy."

"I'll be busy tomorrow," promised Phoebe. "Today I want to smell the flowers and have a good time."

But tomorrow came and

Phoebe was still smelling the flowers and having a good time.

"I'll work tomorrow," said Phoebe.

Every day the bees made honey. They worked all summer long. They didn't have time for anything else. They didn't have time to smell the flowers. They didn't have time to have a good time.

Phoebe kept putting off working.

"You'll be sorry," said the other bees. "You'll be sorry that you always put off until tomorrow what you should be doing today."

"What's so great about doing it today?" asked Phoebe. "Tomorrow will be just as good. Better, probably."

Finally the bees had finished making the honey.

"We're glad we're finished with our job," said the bees. "We're glad we didn't put off working, the way Phoebe did."

That night a little bear came and ate all the honey.

So the next day the bees had to start all over again.

Phoebe smiled as she smelled the flowers and had a good time.

"I'm glad I kept putting off until tomorrow what I should have been doing all along," said Phoebe.

Cyril

Cyril and Jennifer were
squirrels.

They lived in the forest.

Cyril was very, very, very
selfish.

That wasn't very nice. You're supposed to *share*. Jennifer shared. But not Cyril.

"Hey, can I have some of your nuts?" one of the other squirrels would ask Jennifer.

"Help yourself," Jennifer would say.

"Hey, can I have some of your nuts?" one of the other squirrels would ask Cyril.

"Drop dead," Cyril would say.

"You're selfish, Cyril," the other squirrels would say. "You're supposed to share, the way Jennifer does."

Jennifer kept giving her nuts to

the other squirrels. Cyril was too selfish. He kept all of his nuts to himself.

"Hey, can I have some of your nuts, Jennifer?" asked Cyril.

"Help yourself," said Jennifer.

Winter came. Jennifer had given all of her nuts away.

"Hey, can I have some of your nuts, Cyril?" asked Jennifer.

"Drop dead," said Cyril.

And she did.

"I'm glad I was selfish," said

Cyril. "It pays."

Muriel

ALL THE COWS WERE VERY

happy at the farm. And no wonder.

The farmer and his wife were kind,

and the grass was very green. The

cows could eat green grass all day

long. Who could ask for anything more?

Muriel.

Muriel was discontented. "Look how green the grass is on the other side of the fence," Muriel said. "That farm looks nicer than this one."

"This one is nice," said the other cows, chewing the nice green grass.

"And look at that big white

farmhouse over there. Its windows

must be made of diamonds," said

Muriel. "See how they shine."

"It's just the sun shining on the windows that makes them look like diamonds," said the other cows, happily chewing their nice green grass. "Try to be contented, Muriel," they said.

"That farmer is probably so rich he'd give me a diamond collar," said Muriel. "Anyway, that grass is certainly greener than this grass. I'm going over there."

So Muriel started off alone.

All the other cows kept chewing their nice green grass and being contented.

Muriel walked and walked and walked.

She kept walking and walking and walking and walking and finally she reached the other farm.

"Why, the grass *is* greener here," said Muriel. "It's the greenest grass in the world." And it was.

She looked at the big white farmhouse.

"And the windows *are* made of diamonds," she said. And they were.

The new farmer and his wife were very, very kind and very, very rich. The farmer brushed Muriel's coat every day. The farmer's wife gave Muriel a diamond collar.

"It pays to be discontented," said Muriel, as she chewed the greenest, juiciest grass in the world.

Sally

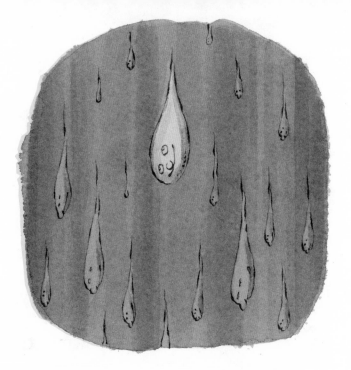

SALLY WAS SLOW.

All the other raindrops were fast. They were always on time. When it was time to rain, they rained.

But not Sally. She was always slow. She was always way, way behind the other raindrops.

The others were always saying, "Hurry, Sally, Hurry! It's time to rain!"

But Sally was always late.

One day all the rain- drops in the cloud with

Sally said, "Come on! It's time to rain! Hurry, Sally! Let's go!"

Every raindrop in the cloud jumped down. But not Sally. Only Sally was left in the cloud, so by then it was a very small cloud indeed.

"Hurry up, slowpoke!" called the other raindrops.

Finally Sally jumped down. She landed on a windowpane.

All the other raindrops were

already racing down the pane.

"Hurry, Sally, hurry," they said as they hurried down the window-pane and jumped into a big mud puddle.

Sally trickled slowly and

dreamily down the pane, peeking

through to see what was going on

inside. She zigged and she zagged.

"You're late again! Hurry!"

called the other raindrops.

But Sally was so slow coming down the pane that finally the sun came out. Sally could feel the warm sun drying her. It felt so good.

Slowly the sun dried Sally and drew her up, up, up into a beautiful rainbow.

Sally looked down at the other raindrops in the big mud puddle.

It pays to be slow, thought Sally.

Gretchen

GRETCHEN WAS GREEDY.

All the other little fish had good manners. All the other little fish ate only what they should, and no more.

But not Gretchen. Gretchen was too greedy. She was always the first one to rush to the table at mealtime and she was always the last one to leave. She loved to eat. "It keeps my spirits up," said Gretchen.

One day Gretchen kept sitting and eating long, long after all the other little fish had excused themselves and left the table. She had five helpings of seaweed salad and seven helpings of kelp cakes.

By that time Gretchen could hardly swim. She floated around, thinking she should exercise or she wouldn't feel like having supper that night, and that would be really terrible.

While she was floating around she saw a worm on a hook. There it was, right in front of her, and it looked particularly delicious.

Now Gretchen really loved

worms. More than seaweed salad,
more than kelp cakes, Gretchen
loved worms. But she had eaten
so much that she didn't have room

for one more bite—even a bite of a worm.

My big chance to eat a nice juicy worm, thought Gretchen sadly, *but I was too greedy at lunch.*

So she swam away from the worm on the hook.

All the other little fish, who had not been as greedy as Gretchen, saw the worm on the hook. And they saw lots of other worms on other hooks.

"Oh, good!" they said. "We're glad *we're* still hungry. We're glad

we weren't greedy at lunchtime, like Gretchen."

So all the other little fish were caught by fishermen that day.

That night Gretchen sat alone at the table. She ate her own dinner, and then she went around the table eating the dinners of all the other little fish.

"It pays to be greedy," sighed Gretchen happily.

Chester

CHESTER WAS LAZY.

Chester was the *laziest* turkey
you ever heard of.

The other turkeys were always
very busy doing whatever it is that

all good turkeys should be doing.

But not Chester. He was too lazy.

He was too lazy to get out of bed.

"What would I do if I *did* get up?" he asked.

"Make your bed," said the other turkeys, who always made theirs.

"What's the use? I'm only going to get right back in it again," said Chester.

As you see, he was very lazy.

If he was inside, he was too lazy to go outside.

If he was outside, he was too lazy to go inside.

He was too lazy to go "gobble gobble." And all turkeys go "gobble gobble."

One chilly morning the farmer called the turkeys.

"Here turkey, turkey, turkey, turkey, turkey!" called the farmer.

All the other turkeys got ready

to run to the farmer to see what he

wanted. "Come on, Chester," said the other turkeys.

"I'm going to stay in bed," said Chester.

"You're so lazy, Chester. How will you know what the farmer wants?" asked the other turkeys.

"Come back and tell me," yawned Chester.

"Lazybones," said the other turkeys. They all ran to see what it was the farmer wanted.

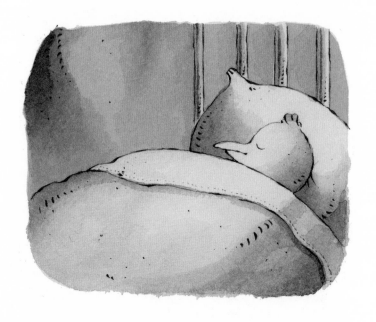

The next morning, which was Thanksgiving morning, Chester looked around the empty barn. *It pays to be lazy*, thought Chester, turning over for a little nap.

Annette

ALL THE LITTLE MONKEYS were just finishing breakfast when the father monkey said, "Remember, today is the day we're going to put up a nice new swing.

We'll hang it from the highest tree."

"Oh, good," said all the little monkeys.

"But first we'll have to pick all of the coconuts and pile them in neat little piles," said the father monkey. "Then after we've done all of our work, we can swing and swing."

Annette sighed. *I hate to pick coconuts and pile them in neat little piles*, she thought.

Then she said, "I feel sick."
That was not true. "I feel terrible,"
she said. *That* was true. She felt

terrible because she was afraid she was going to have to pick coconuts and pile them in neat little piles.

"Oh dear," said the mother monkey. "Then you'll have to go to bed, dear."

So Annette went to bed.

"How do you feel now, dear?" asked the mother monkey.

"Terrible," said Annette. That was not true. "I think I'd feel better if you'd read to me." *That* was

true. Annette loved to have her
mother read to her.

The mother monkey read to Annette. She read seven books. "How do you feel now, dear?" she asked Annette.

"I think I'd feel better if I had something to eat," said Annette. That was true. Annette loved to eat.

So the mother monkey brought Annette a nice banana and some coconut milk.

"How do you feel now, dear?" asked the mother monkey.

"I think I'd feel better if I had a

softer bed," said Annette. That was

true.

So the mother monkey asked

the father monkey and the little monkeys to bring soft leaves and branches to make a new bed for Annette. Then they went back to work picking coconuts. Annette stayed in her soft bed.

Finally the coconuts were all picked and piled in neat little piles.

Finally the swing was hung from the highest tree.

The father monkey and the little monkeys were so tired from doing all that work that they couldn't even eat their nice bananas and drink their coconut milk. They were too tired to play on the swing. They went to bed.

"How do you feel now, dear?" the mother monkey asked Annette.

"Terrible," said Annette. That

was true. "I think I'd feel better if I went outside and got some fresh air."

So Annette went outside.

"It pays to know when to tell the truth," said Annette to herself, as she swung back and forth on the new swing.

Caleb
&
Conrad

CALEB AND CONRAD WERE
brothers.

Their parents had taught them
to be polite and kind and thoughtful and gracious and truthful.

One day their mother spent all morning scrubbing the kitchen floor. She was a very neat and industrious person.

She called to Caleb and Conrad, who were outside making mud

balls. "If anyone steps on my nice clean floor, his name will be mud," she called firmly. She was a very firm person.

Then she went upstairs to take a bath. She was a person who spent a lot of time in the bathtub.

Caleb and Conrad kept working on the mud balls until they had enough to last for six days. They were very thirsty.

"I'll go in and get us a drink of

water," said Caleb, who was a very kind and thoughtful person.

"Oh, don't bother, I'll get it," said Conrad.

"Oh, all right, then, you get it,"

said Caleb graciously. Caleb was a very gracious person.

So Conrad went into the kitchen and brought out a nice glass of cold water.

When their mother came down-
stairs after her bath and saw the
kitchen floor, she came outside to
visit with Caleb and Conrad.

"Who tracked mud all over my nice clean floor?" asked their mother.

"I did," said Conrad truthfully. *It pays to be truthful*, thought Conrad.

Conrad was wrong.

The End

FLORENCE PARRY HEIDE

(1919–2011) was the author of more than one hundred children's books, including picture books, juvenile novels, two series of young-adult mysteries, plays, songbooks, and poetry. She may be best remembered for her now-classic *The Shrinking of Treehorn* and its two sequels, illustrated by the great Edward Gorey. Florence grew up in Punxsutawney, Pennsylvania, married during the Second World War, and spent her adult life in Kenosha, Wisconsin, with her husband and five children, all of whom grew up listening to the joyful sounds of an old typewriter.

SYLVIA WORTH VAN CLIEF

(1920–1974) collaborated with Florence on hundreds of songs for both children and adults, as well as many books, including a series of sports-themed young-adult novels and several titles in the Spotlight Club Mystery series.

SERGIO RUZZIER has written
and illustrated many picture books. He was
awarded the Sendak Fellowship in 2011. Born
in Italy, he lives in Brooklyn, New York. Visit
Sergio online at Ruzzier.com.

SERGIO RUZZIER has written and illustrated many picture books. He was awarded the Sendak Fellowship in 2011. Born in Italy, he lives in Brooklyn, New York. Visit Sergio online at Ruzzier.com.